S0-AJT-163

The Undersea Adventures of
DIGBY DOLPHIN

Written by
Drue DeMatteis

Illustrated by
Sarah Smith

Digby Dolphin was always ready for an adventure. He lived in Rainbow Reef, a colorful patch of coral that was home to many undersea creatures. One of those creatures was Digby's best friend, Prickly Pufferfish. Prickly wasn't so adventurous.

One day Digby and Prickly were playing a game of hide-and-go-seek. Rainbow Reef had plenty of great hiding spots, and since Prickly was small he always found the best places to hide.

"Ready or not, here I come!" yelled Digby, whose strong tail and smooth skin made him one of the fastest swimmers in the sea.

Prickly had gone inside a hole in the coral, a hole so dark that it made each spine on his body quiver with fear. "Maybe I should find another hiding place," Prickly said to himself.

But as he started to leave the hole, he heard a breathing sound: HUH-uh, HUH-uh. The noise began to grow louder and louder!

Prickly swam for the exit, but before he got out of the hole he was stopped by these words: "Find . . . Princess . . . Iris."

"P-P-Princess wh-who?" Prickly asked, squinting his eyes into the darkness. He could see a shape now, and it was moving slowly toward him, getting closer. While Prickly peered into the hole, something came behind him.

"GOTCHA!" yelled Digby.

"Aaagghh!" Prickly screamed, spinning around to see his friend laughing.

"Hey, what's going on?" asked Digby, poking his nose near the hole.

The mysterious shape Prickly had been watching now moved from the darkness. It was a sea horse.

"My name is Sarah," said the breathless sea horse. "I am the guardian of Iris, the angelfish princess of Rainbow Reef. I need your help."

Digby and Prickly listened as Sarah told them her story. Princess Iris had been carried away from Rainbow Reef by a strong current and was now trapped in the Sea of Jelly. The Sea of Jelly was a beautiful part of the sea, but it was also dangerous. Thousands of jellyfish floated there.

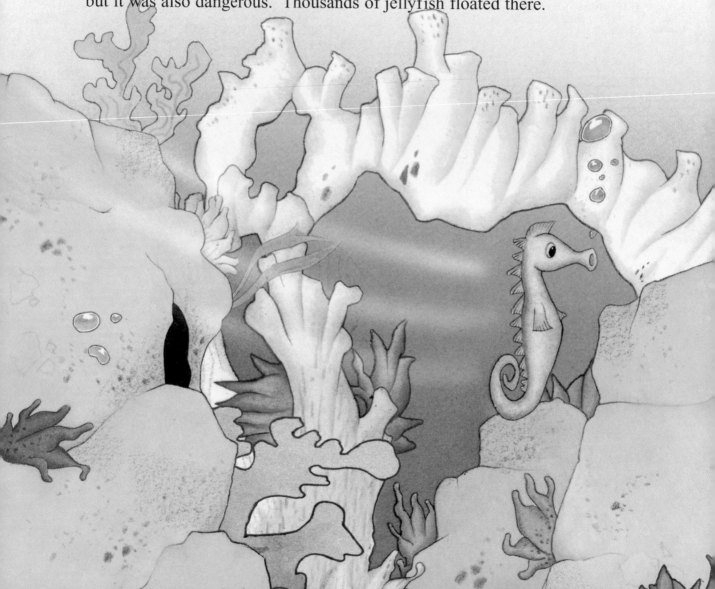

"Please help me rescue Princess Iris," Sarah Seahorse pleaded. "I'm too tired to swim anymore. Return her to Rainbow Reef and you'll be rewarded."

Digby's tail fin twitched with excitement; now here was an adventure! Prickly, however, started to puff up again. He didn't like what he'd heard. "The Sea of Jelly is too dangerous," he said. "We'll never make it."

"There is a way," Sarah told them, "but it's a long and difficult journey. I can't go with you, but I can tell you where to start."

"Tell us," said Digby, winking at his fearful little friend. "We can do it."

"You must go to Hueless Hollow," said Sarah, "and find Otis Octopus."

Hueless Hollow was far away from Rainbow Reef. To get there, Digby and Prickly had to swim for a long time. On their journey they swam past other coral reefs. They swam above deep ocean gulches. And they met up and swam with colorful schools of fish.

Eventually they arrived at a place that looked like an underwater desert. There were hills of sugary sand and smooth, colorless stones.

"Not a good place for hide-and-go-seek," said Digby.

Prickly agreed. But that gave him an idea.

"Tag, you're it!" Prickly shouted, darting away from Digby. Digby smiled at his friend who was swimming toward the sea floor.

"Alright, you're on," Digby said, and the chase began.

Turning to look behind him, Prickly laughed. Digby was getting closer. Suddenly, Prickly swam smack into what looked like a rock.

"Yeeeowwch!" it yelled.

And that's how Digby and Prickly met Otis Octopus.

"What're you boys doin' in Hueless Holler?" grumbled the octopus, pulling pufferfish thorns from his side.

"We're trying to rescue Princess Iris," Digby said quickly. "Are you Otis Octopus?"

Now, the octopus looked amused. "Ahm Otis," he said, "but ah don't believe ah know any *Prinsuss Ahrus*."

Then Prickly spoke up. "She's a beautiful angelfish from Rainbow Reef and she's trapped in the Sea of Jelly and Sarah Seahorse asked us to save her, but we had to find you first because maybe you know how to get through the Sea of Jelly!"

"Ah see," said Otis, a bit puzzled.   Then he stared at Digby and Prickly for a bit. "Tell you boys what," he finally said. "Ah don't know any Prinsuss Ahrus, ah don't know any Sarah Seahorse and ah certainly don't know you two. But my reputation for good deeds must be well-known." That said, Otis pulled a necklace made of shells from beneath a rock. "Take this to that sunken ship over yonder. There's a magic starfish inside. She'll help you. But be careful now, bubs. Some mean hammerhead sharks swim 'round that ship—and they bite!

Digby and Prickly thanked Otis and then swam away with the necklace.

From a distance, Digby and Prickly watched as four hammerhead sharks swam circles around the sunken ship. Prickly started to puff up from fear.

"I have a plan," whispered Digby. "I'm going to trick the sharks. When they go away, we swim to the ship."

"B-but, what if I d-don't swim f-fast enough?" asked Prickly.

"Don't worry," said Digby. "We'll be okay." Then he yelled, "Look, behind the ship, a school of *nail*fish!"

The hammerheads went behind the ship and the two friends took off. But poor Prickly was so scared that his body inflated like a balloon. He couldn't keep up with Digby, who was already at the ship!

Realizing they'd been tricked, the hammerheads turned around and saw Prickly.

"Pufferfish for lunch!" they shouted.

Just as the sharks were about to get him, Prickly was swept away in a flash! It was Digby, pushing his friend to safety through a hole in the ship.

"WOW!" Prickly yelled. "What a great rescue! What a getaway! Those hammerheads looked like fools—HA!"

"Shhhhhhh," whispered Digby. "Listen."

Inside the creaky old ship, Digby and Prickly could hear a voice. Quietly, they swam down a dark hall and then up a narrow stairway until they came to a door. A soft and soothing singing sound came from behind it.

La-la-la-la-la-la-laah
Lo-lo-lo-lo-lo-lo-looo
Lu-lu-lu-lu-lu-lu-laah
La-ta-ta-tee-tee-dee-daah.

Nudging the door open, Digby and Prickly saw a bright orange starfish
twirling on a steering wheel while swirling ribbons of seaweed in her arms.
"Are you the magic starfish?" Digby asked.
Still spinning, the starfish answered:

That's who I am, with five arms that spin;
Don't be afraid, please come on in.

"We need you to help us," Digby told the starfish. "Princess Iris of Rainbow Reef is trapped in the Sea of Jelly. Can you help us get to her?"

You've come looking for help, now isn't that nice,
But my magic's not free, it comes with a price.

Digby swam to the magic starfish and gave her the necklace Otis had given them. The starfish put it on, and with a happy smile she began to chant,

Spin-around, spin-around, in a whirlpool we'll whisk,
To the Sea of Jelly, to save Princess Iris.

Safe inside a whirlpool tunnel, Digby, Prickly and the magic starfish were sucked straight to the Sea of Jelly. There, jellyfish floated in the water at every depth, but their stinging tentacles could not reach inside the tunnel.

Before they knew it, Digby and Prickly were underneath a rock ledge, face to face with a beautiful angelfish. They had found Princess Iris.

"Have you come to save me?" she asked.

"Yes, Princess Iris," said Digby. "Sarah Seahorse told us you were here. We're taking you back to Rainbow Reef."

And with another swirl of her arms, the magic starfish whipped up a whirlpool tunnel. In no time at all, everyone was whisked back to Rainbow Reef.

Sarah Seahorse nearly fainted. "My Princess!" she gasped. "They saved you!"

Digby and Prickly were the heroes of Rainbow Reef! All the fish, crabs and creatures who lived near the reef came for a grand celebration.

"Wasn't this a great adventure?" Digby asked.

Prickly smiled at his friend. He had to agree.

As a token of her thanks, Princess Iris gave Digby a lovely reward—a sand dollar necklace. And Prickly? He got the nicest present of all—a kiss from the beautiful princess!

Boy did he puff up!